MYRON'S MAGIC COW

To Michael Austin, wherever he is, who brought
Myron to life on the stage of Trinity Elementary School.
And to all the children in my charge in
all my years of teaching – M. N.

For my lovely wife, Alex – J.

Barefoot Books
124 Walcot Street
Bath BA1 5BG

This book has been printed on 100% acid-free paper
The illustrations were prepared digitally, using a mixture
of scanned, painted, drawn and photographed sources
Design by Louise Millar, London
Typeset in Aunt Mildred
Colour separation by Grafiscan, Verona
Printed and bound in Singapore
by Tien Wah Press Pte Ltd

Hardback ISBN 1-84148-495-4

British Cataloguing-in-Publication Data:
a catalogue record for this book
is available from the British Library

1 3 5 7 9 8 6 4 2

Acknowledgements
I would like to acknowledge the people who have supported my efforts and given me
most valuable criticism. They include Candace Whitman, Rolaine Hochstein,
Deyva Arthur, Jody and Cecilia MacDonald, Nancy Lynk, Sue Miller, Eric Luper
and all the members of the Capital District Society of Children's Book Writers
and Illustrators, and, of course, my loving family – M. N.

MYRON'S MAGIC COW

written by Marlene Newman

illustrated by Jago

Barefoot Books
Celebrating Art and Story

Whenever Mum needed something, Will was too busy and Rita was too little to help, so it was always Myron who was sent to the shops.

Like last Sunday morning, when Mum decided to make pancakes for breakfast. She got out her bowl, spoon, measuring jug and frying pan. She took out the flour, eggs and the carton of milk ... but the milk was all gone.

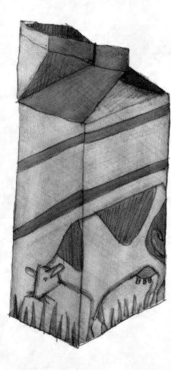

'I need milk for the pancakes!' she called.
'Myron, take some money out of my bag and run
down to the shops.'

And so, as usual, Myron had to go. Out of the
flat, down the corridor, into the lift, through the
entrance hall and up the busy street he went.

'Pssst!' Myron heard a peculiar sound.

'Pssst!'

There it was again.

Myron turned the corner. Once more he heard an insistent 'Pssst!' from the alleyway that separated two tall buildings.

He looked over his shoulder and saw a girl with curly, blonde hair holding a rope.

'Listen,' the girl whispered. 'I hear there's no milk at your house.'

Myron knew that he wasn't supposed to talk to strangers, and this was certainly no one he knew.

How could she know they were out of milk?

'Listen,' she repeated. 'I've got something for you. You'll never have to go to the shops to buy milk again.'

The girl tugged at the rope, and dragged a huge cow out of the alley and on to the street.

'What do you think of her?' she asked. 'A dopey boy who said his name was Jack has just swapped her for a pack of mouldy old beans I had. Quite a good deal, wasn't it?'

Now Myron had seen pictures of cows in books and on cartoons, on TV and in films. But he had never ever before been face to face with a real live cow. He was speechless.

'Listen,' the girl continued. 'There are already three bears in my car and the cow just won't fit. You need milk and I need money — so let's talk. How much cash do you have on you?'

Myron pinched himself to see if he was awake. Then he opened his hand and looked at the wrinkled note.

'Myron, this is your lucky day! That's exactly how much the cow will cost you.' The girl snatched the money out of Myron's hand and gave him the rope.

Before Myron could say 'Yes', 'No' or 'Maybe', the girl jumped into the back of her car. The bear at the wheel revved the engine and they vanished down the street in a cloud of smelly black smoke.

Myron wondered what his Mum would say ... what his Mum would do when he returned home with this extremely large container of milk. Well, at least it would be better than no milk at all. Myron looked at the cow. The cow looked back at Myron. Neither of them was particularly happy to be at the opposite end of the same rope.

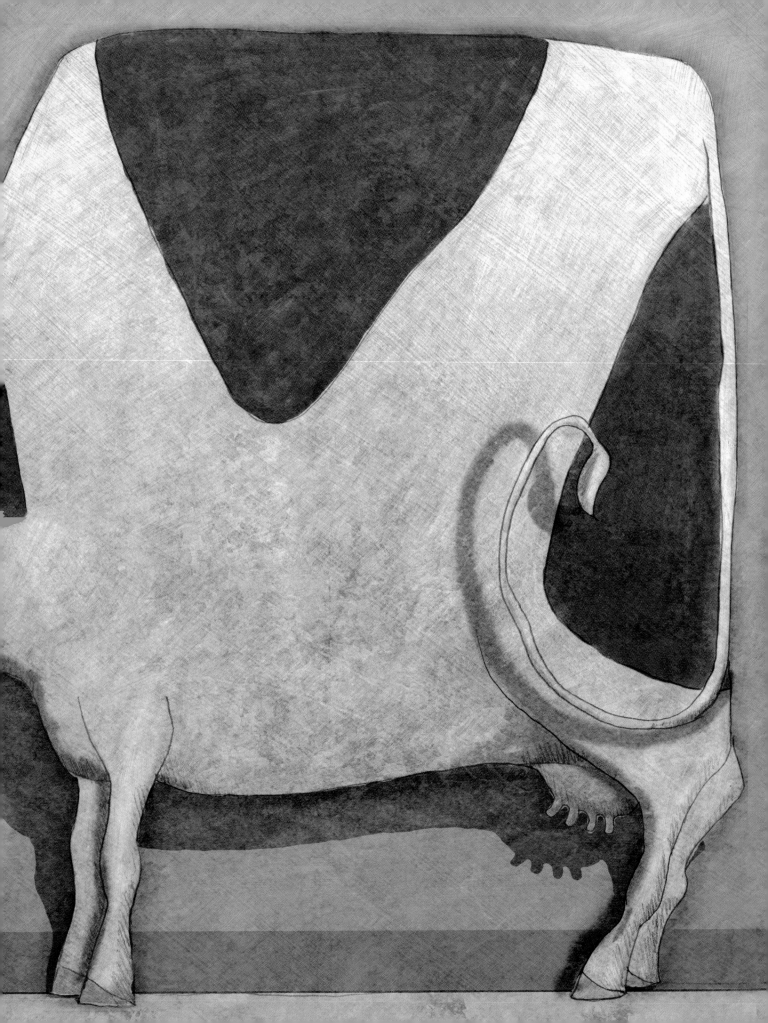

People on the street were staring. Some whispered to each other. Others laughed. And still others shouted insults.

Myron tugged at the rope. The cow plopped down on the pavement and made a loud, unpleasant noise.

'Look at that boy with the enormous cow!' someone cried. And Myron cried, too.

He grabbed the rope with both hands and pulled as hard as he could. This time the cow stood up and Myron sat down – with a hard bump.

He got to his feet and pulled again. The cow moved.
Myron pulled again. The cow came closer. Myron took a
step. So did the cow. Myron walked up the street.
The cow followed. They walked past the supermarket, the
bakery, the video shop, the playground and the school.

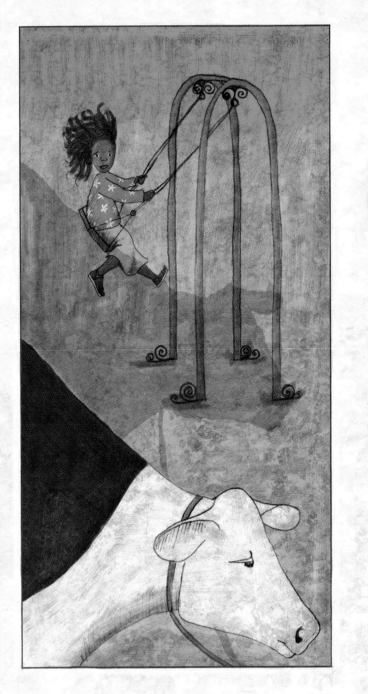 

Myron tried to behave as if it was perfectly normal to be
pulling a cow down the street on a Sunday morning.

And so, pushing and pulling, stopping and starting,
they struggled along until they reached the block of flats
where Myron lived.

'Here we are,' said Myron.

The cow nodded and came to a stop. Myron pressed the
button to get in, but nothing happened.

'Open sesame!' said the cow, and the door swung open.

Myron spun round in astonishment, and the cow gave

him a nudge. 'Hurry up, or it will shut again.'

'I don't understand.'

'What don't you understand? Open sesame?'

Myron understood the words well enough. He just couldn't believe where they were coming from.

'Excuse me,' he said. 'I didn't know cows could talk.'

'Don't tell anyone. We've always been able to talk. But as long as no one knows, we can listen in on all kinds of things. I've been around, you know, and I've picked up a few tricks here and there. Learnt that one from my old pal Ali Baba. What's your floor?'

The lift rattled up to the fifth floor. Myron still didn't know what to tell his Mum. The door of the lift slid open. Myron pulled the rope. The cow wouldn't budge. A little light flashed on. Myron got behind the cow and shoved her out just as the lift door closed behind them.

He started down the long hall, pulling and tugging at
his end of the rope as the cow pulled and tugged at hers.
Still pulling and pushing, Myron fumbled with his key
and opened the door.

'Myron,' his Mum called. 'Is that you? Did you get the milk?'

'Sort of,' Myron mumbled.

'What? I can't hear you. How many times have I told you
to open your mouth and speak clearly? Where's the milk?
I can't make pancakes without milk. Myron ... come on ...
it's almost lunchtime and we still haven't had breakfast.'

'I'm coming,' Myron answered. But he was hunting
through the toy chest for his old plastic bucket.

'If I can get enough milk for the pancakes,' he thought,
'then I'll have time to work out what to tell her.'

'Myron … I'm waiting. What's the matter? Can't you
bring the milk in here?'

'I'll be there in a minute, Mum.'

Myron found the plastic bucket. He put it under the cow and began to squeeze and pull and squeeze and pull.

Nothing happened. He squeezed and pulled and squeezed again. Still nothing happened. Myron was close to tears. He stood up and looked the cow straight in the eye.

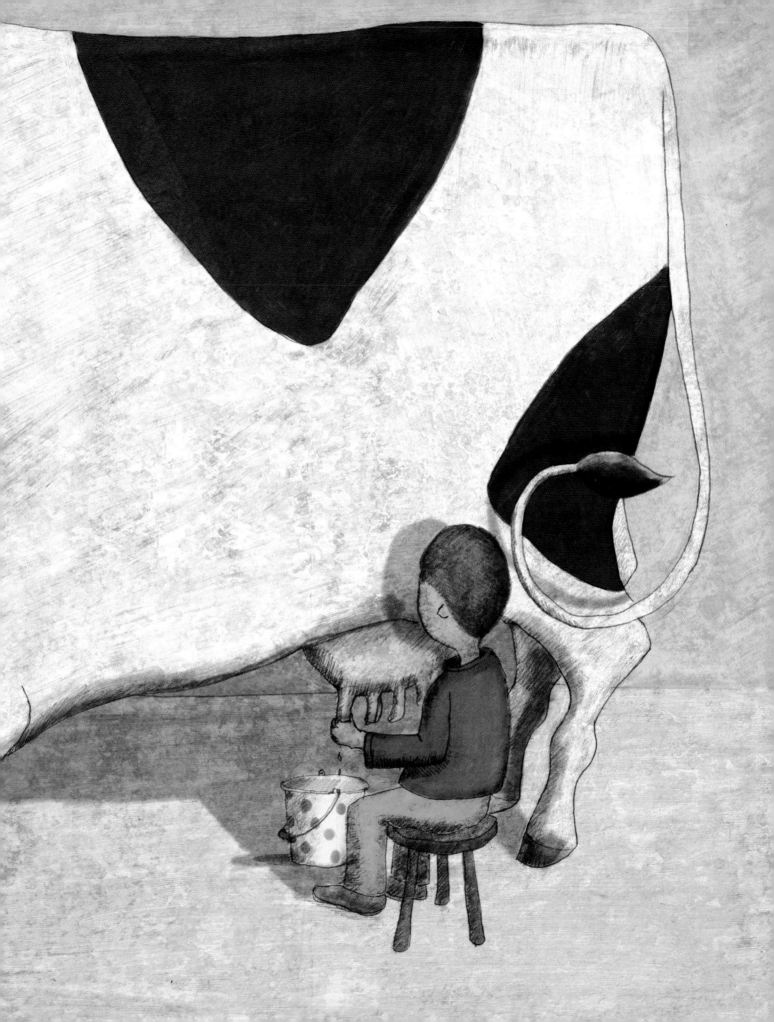

'Listen,' he said to her. 'I'm sorry about this, but I'm not
happy either. I wish you would co-operate — then maybe I'll
find a way out of this for both of us. Please ...'

'Since you put it that way.'

'What?'

'The magic word.'

'What?'

'You know ... the magic word ... please — the magic word.'

'I don't understand.'

'Which word don't you understand? Magic? Please?'

'Both ... I mean neither ... I mean please — please could you help me?'

The cow gave a superior smile.

'You humans are all the same. You have no idea what we animals can do. Still, at least you helped me get away from that awful girl. Never trust blondes, that's what I say, especially when they're girls travelling with bears. Who knows what they might have done to me if you hadn't walked by? I owe you a favour. What would you like — full, semi-skimmed or skimmed?'

'Whatever,' Myron answered, too flustered to decide.

He squeezed again and his plastic bucket filled with fresh, creamy milk.

'Thank you,' he said as he raced with it into the kitchen.

The cow was looking around the flat when Myron returned with the empty bucket.

'That should do it for now,' he said. 'But I still don't know how to explain this to my Mum.'

'Look,' the cow replied. 'I don't just give milk. I can do other things too.'

'Like what?'

'Ever heard of genies?'

'You mean ...'

'Yes, that's exactly what I mean.'

'Do I get three wishes?'

'You've already used one. Remember ... the milk?'

'I'd better be careful. Let me see. I wish I wasn't so
nervous. I'd be able to think better.'

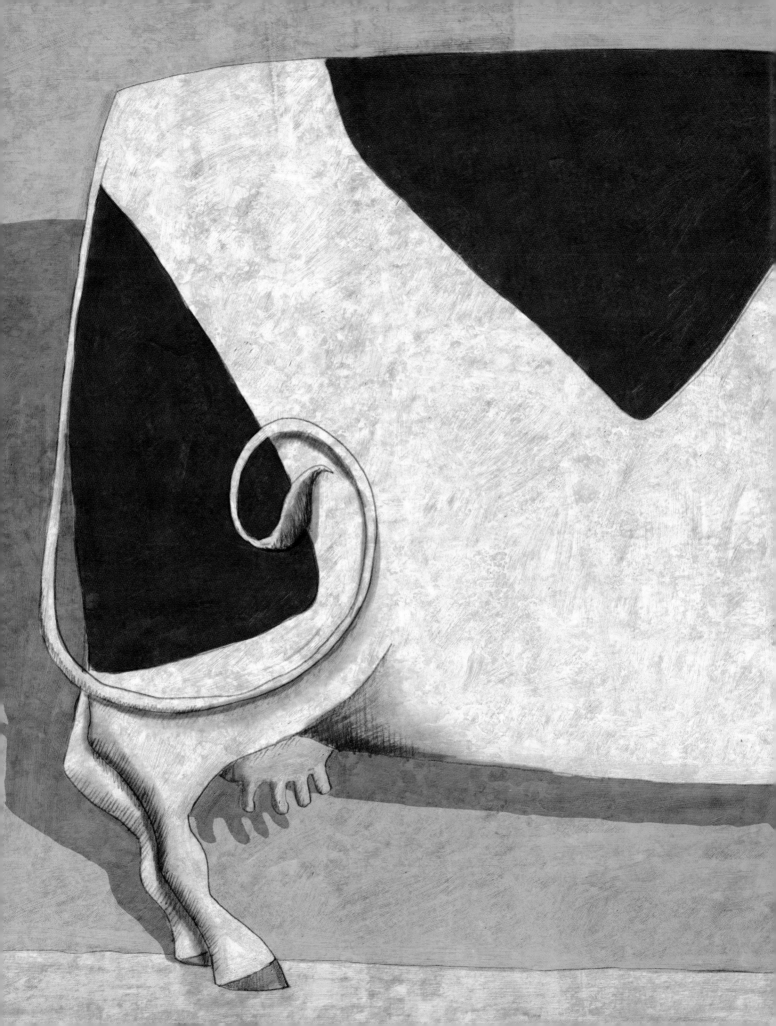

And a calm he had never felt before came over Myron as the cow exclaimed, 'Two! One more to go.'

Myron could think clearly now. He was certain he would make a wise wish. He put his arms around the cow and said, 'I wish someone else would have to go to the shops once in a while.'

'Done!'

And a calm he had never felt before came over Myron as the cow exclaimed, 'Two! One more to go.'

Myron could think clearly now. He was certain he would make a wise wish. He put his arms around the cow and said, 'I wish someone else would have to go to the shops once in a while.'

'Done!'

A great flash of light filled the room, and when it had passed, the cow had vanished.

Mum called from the kitchen, 'Pancakes will be ready soon. Will, go to the shops for some golden syrup — and get another pack of eggs while you're there, could you?'

Myron heaved a long, happy sigh and smiled all the way down to the tips of his toes.

Then he looked down at the floor — was that an egg?

He'd never seen such a big egg in his life.

It was shiny, too. Could it be ... a golden egg?